Eddie's Garden

and How to Make Things Grow

Sarah Garland

FRANCES LINCOLN CHILDREN'S BOOKS

for
Flora Blossom
with love

"Can I have a garden of my own?" said Eddie.
"Okay," said Mum.

"And me," said Lily.

Mum wrote a list

and they went to the garden shop.

They bought seeds,
and a bag of earth,
and some flowerpots.

"Pots for me,"
said Lily.

"What makes plants grow?" asked Eddie.
"What makes you grow?" asked Mum.
"Food," said Eddie.
"Drink for me," said Lily.
"That's just what plants like,"
said Mum.

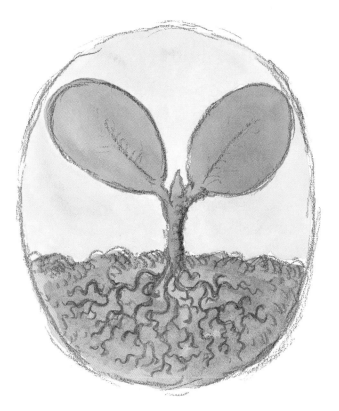

"Food from the earth,

rain to drink,

air to breathe,

and sun for light and warmth."

"Let's get digging," said Eddie.

It was hard work digging up the grass and weeds, but the earth was rich and crumbly and full of worms.

"Stop that, Lily!" cried Mum. "Worms are good for the earth but they are not good to eat!"

"Worms for me," said Lily.

Eddie raked the earth smooth,
ready for the pea seeds.

Mum showed Eddie how to scratch a line
in the earth with a twig,

and how to put the pea seeds
in along the line, one at a time,

and carefully cover them up.

They collected some long sticks and Mum pushed them into the ground.

"This can be a hide-out for you and Lily," she said. "Bean plants will grow right up the sticks to make you a bean den."

She dug a hole beside each stick, and Eddie dropped a bean into every hole, and filled each hole with earth.

Eddie watered all the seeds
with his watering can.

"Water me," said Lily.

"No, DON'T!"
said Mum.

When Eddie went to bed
that night, Mum read him the story
of *Jack and the Beanstalk*.

Eddie thought about his bean plants
growing up into the sky, and how he would
be like Jack and climb up the beanstalk,
higher and higher, until he could
touch the clouds.

Next morning, Eddie wanted to sow more seeds.

"Let's put some of these in pots," said Mum.
"Then we can look after them more easily."

So they collected flowerpots, seed trays, yoghurt pots,
an oil can, and one old boot, and filled them with earth from
the bag. Eddie watered the earth until it was soaking wet.

Then they chose their seeds – sunflower and marigold
seeds, nasturtiums and broccoli,
purple chard and sweetcorn,
and a pumpkin seed for Lily.

They put in their seeds carefully
and covered them up with earth.

"Pumpkin for me," said Lily, and she dug up
her pumpkin seed to see whether it had grown.
"Put it back, Lily! It doesn't grow
that fast!" said Eddie.

Days passed. The rain rained and the sun shone warm.

Every day Eddie and Lily looked to see whether their seeds had sprouted.

At last a strong green stem pushed out of the earth. It was Lily's pumpkin plant! It straightened up and opened two fat leaves.

"Like me!" said Lily.

Soon all the seeds were sprouting.

Eddie worked hard in his garden.

He watered the plants when they were dry, and he pulled up the weeds.

When Lily's pumpkin plant grew too big for its pot, he showed her how to dig a hole in the garden to plant it in, so its roots could go down deep into the ground.

"Hey, Lily. Maybe that hole is a bit too big," said Eddie.

Then he dug a hole
for his sunflower plant, right
in the middle of the garden.

As the weeks
went by, it
grew as high
as Eddie.

Then even higher,
and higher still,
until a fat bud
grew at the top,

which opened out
into an enormous
yellow sunflower.

Grandad came round.
He was so surprised, he had to sit down.
"Wow, Eddie! Your garden is amazing!" he said.

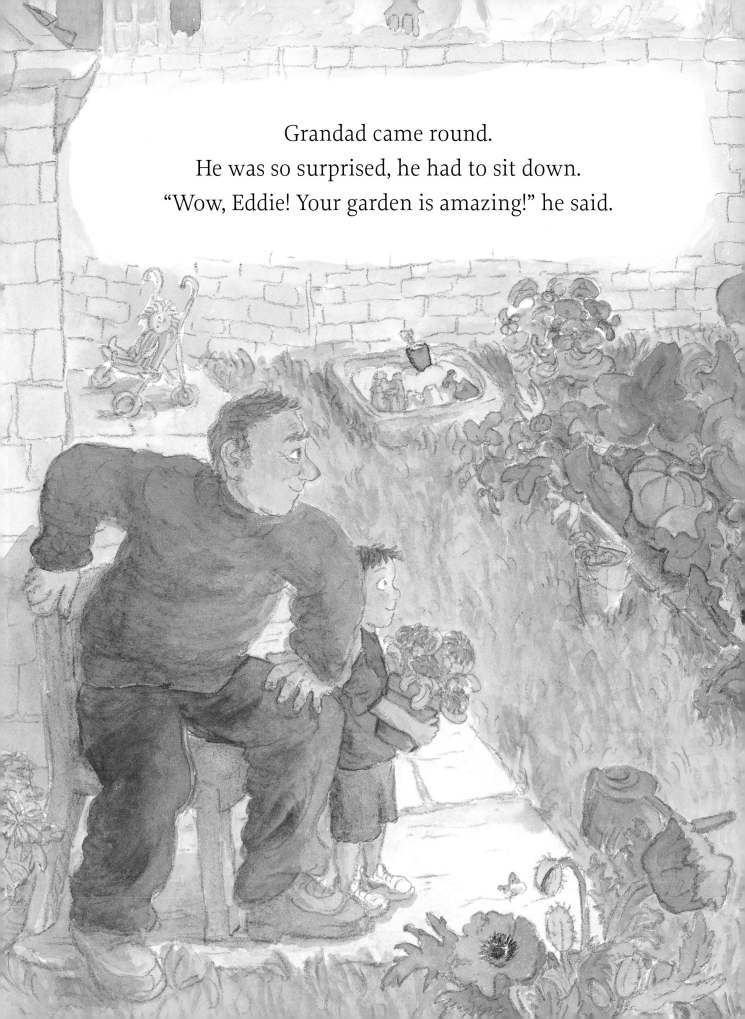

They walked around the garden together.
"Do you know what, Grandad?" said Eddie.

"Some caterpillars
eat lettuces but birds
eat caterpillars.

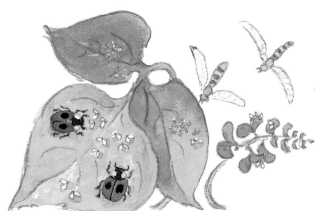

And some bugs eat leaves
and flowers, but ladybirds
and hoverflies eat the bugs.

And bees make honey
from flowers, and we like
eating honey."

"Worms for me," said Lily.
"Well, worms mix the earth up,
and that's good for plants," said Grandad.

Eddie found a slug.

"Oh dear," said Grandad. "Slugs eat up plants in the garden, especially at night."

"Uh-oh!" said Eddie.

That night Eddie couldn't sleep.

He kept thinking about slugs
munching and crunching in his garden.

He went downstairs in his pyjamas.

"What's up, Eddie?" called Mum.

"I'm going on a slug hunt," said Eddie.

"Wait for me," said Mum.

By torchlight and moonlight they
soon found sixteen slugs that were
eating up Eddie's plants. They put
them in a bucket for Mum to throw
away, and went back upstairs.

"That was a brilliant idea, Eddie,"
said Mum, as she kissed him good night.

The next day was fine and sunny,
perfect for a picnic.

   Eddie, Lily and Mum went out into the garden
and picked peas and carrots and lettuces and
sweetcorn, and a big pumpkin.

Mum cut the pumpkin up.

"We'll keep some of these seeds to grow next year," she said.

Eddie rolled out pastry for pumpkin pie.

"Peas for me," said Lily.

Out in Eddie's garden, birds ate sunflower seeds,
bees and butterflies drank nectar from the flowers,
and creepy-crawlies were busy in the earth.

Eddie, Lily, Mum and Grandad ate their picnic.
It was the best ever.

After the picnic, Eddie and Lily sat in the bean den.
"Which do you like best, Lily, worms or beans?"
asked Eddie.

"BEANS FOR ME," said Lily.

How to grow Eddie's plants

CARROTS   Choose seed of short, rounded carrots, which taste sweet and germinate well. If the soil is heavy, add sand to lighten it, and sow seed in mid-spring. Thin plants to 4 cm (1 ½ ins) apart. Eat raw, or lightly cooked with butter and lemon juice.

LETTUCE   Varieties include crisp, hearted lettuces or loose-leaved, red or green, frilly types, whose leaves can be picked one at a time. Sow in early spring indoors in containers, and outside throughout the summer. Thin to 12 – 30 cms (4 ½–11 ½ ins) apart, depending on variety. Keep watered, and watch for slugs.

NASTURTIUMS   Flowers best in a poor soil and sunny position. Sow in mid-spring in containers or outdoors. Leaves, buds and flowers are all edible. Watch out for blackfly.

ONIONS   These are easiest to grow from 'sets' – tiny, immature onions. Plant them 15 cm (6 ins) apart in a sunny position in early spring, with the tips just below soil level. When the leaves die down in late summer, dig up the whole plant gently, and leave to dry before storing.

PEAS   Sow in rich, deep soil, from mid-spring, 3 cm (1 in) deep and 10 cm (4 ins) apart, with twiggy supports or wire for them to climb. Keep picking to encourage production of pods, and water well.

POT MARIGOLD   Sow seeds in mid-spring and give the young plants plenty of space to develop. Sprinkle the pretty flower petals over salads and soups. (Not to be confused with the African and French *Tagetes* marigolds.)

PUMPKIN   Sow seeds in pots indoors and plant out in late spring in a sheltered, warm place, in a rich soil. They will grow enormous leaves, and long stems that can be trained up sticks, or over a fence. Keep watering. Delicious eaten any size, stewed or roasted, and in soups and pies.

RUNNER BEANS   Sow seeds 5 cm (2 ins) deep, 20 cm (8 ins) apart, in rich, deeply dug ground, in late spring when the earth has warmed up. For an earlier start, sow single seeds in pots, or in cardboard tubes of compost that can be planted out later, tubes and all. Keep well watered. Make sure all old beans are picked so plants are encouraged to keep producing tender young beans.

SPROUTING BROCCOLI   Sow in late spring, and put the sturdy plants out 60 cm (23 ins) apart in good, firm soil. Stake well, as they grow a bushy 90 cm (35 ins) high. The shoots can be picked for a month or more, the following spring.

SUNFLOWER   Sow seeds in pots indoors, in mid spring, to give them time to develop a good size. Plant out in late spring in rich soil, in the sun. Keep staking as they grow.

SWEETCORN   Sow single seeds in pots indoors. Plant out in early summer, 36 cm (14 ins) apart, in rich soil, in a sunny, sheltered place.

SWISS CHARD   Choose the handsome Rainbow varieties with their coloured stems. They are very easy to grow and will tolerate heavy soil. Sow in late spring and thin plants 15 cm (6 ins) apart. Pick outer leaves and stems and eat in salads when young, and lightly steamed when older.

The Earth

Always choose the best place in the garden for a plot like Eddie's. However small, it should be in the sunniest, most sheltered, and most encouraging position.

Is the earth thin and dusty, or heavy and dense? It may need enriching and bulking out with bought or home-made manure or compost, or feeding with a concentrated organic fertilizer. Artificial fertilizers may encourage quick growth, but produce softer, weaker plants, and are also a cause of pollution.

Once the earth is dug and raked, try not to tread and compact the soil. Put a plank across the bed to stand on when tending the plants.

Seeds

Most of Eddie's seeds are quite large and easy to handle, and germinate well and quickly. Wait until the ground warms up before sowing seeds outdoors – they won't germinate in cold, wet earth. Most seeds can be sown in furrows and are covered with soil to twice their depth. Sow thinly – seeds cannot survive too much competition. Try to keep seedbeds moist, and water with only the finest spray, or seedlings may be damaged.

Seeds sown in containers indoors or in a greenhouse have a good start as they are protected from cold weather and bugs. Use shop-bought, organic, peat-free compost, and water well before sowing.

Seeds of short-rooted plants are happy in seed trays; those that will develop large roots are best sown singly in pots. To encourage germination, cover containers and leave them in a warm, dark place.  Check them every day, and at the first sign of a shoot, take them into the light, or the plants will become pale and spindly. Leave them on a cool windowsill, turning them daily so they don't lean towards the light. Water from below, by standing the container in water. Put them outside in a sheltered spot when frosts are over. When at least two sets of leaves have formed, plant them out in the garden, holding them gently by the leaves, not by the vulnerable stems. Do this in the evening or on an overcast day and water well.

Container Gardening

All the plants in Eddie's garden can be grown in any strong container. Drainage is important, so sit the container on a layer of gravel or sticks, so water can drain away beneath. Put stones in the bottom of the container and fill with rich, soil-based compost. Keep well watered and feed several times during the summer with an organic fertilizer or a layer of garden compost.

Choose deep containers and use extra fertilizer for big plants like pumpkins, and peas and beans (use dwarf varieties). Lettuce, Swiss chard (when used young for salads), and smaller flowers will grow in shallower pots.

Indoor Gardening

If you cannot grow plants outdoors, then use a sunny windowsill. Keep turning the containers each day so plants don't lean towards the light. Although this limits what you can grow, just a pot of young carrots, or trays of salad seedlings that can be cut with scissors, or a bowl of bulbs, are a real pleasure.

By sprouting seeds indoors, you can watch their developing shoots and roots, and eat them in sandwiches or stir-fries. Use special, untreated seeds. Put a spoonful in an empty jam jar and tie a piece of muslin over the top. Fill with water, leave for half an hour, then tip the water out through the muslin. Keep the jar by the sink and rinse and drain the seeds gently each day until they are sprouted. Alfalfa seed is particularly successful when sprouted this way.

Pests

By keeping a close watch on plants, you can usually keep bugs under control. Squash all blackfly, greenfly and other aphids. Slugs and snails come out at night and after rain, so collect them then, or put out saucers of beer or sugar water, which they will drown in. Avoid using slug pellets if possible.

Birds may eat lettuce and cabbage leaves, and young pea shoots. Protect plants with netting, windmills, or strips of rustling foil.

Bare, raked earth can be enticing to cats, who may scratch up seed-beds and use them as a lavatory. Protect beds with netting or wire until the plants are grown.

Hazards

Everything in Eddie's garden is edible, but it is very important to teach children to ALWAYS check with an adult before eating anything from the garden.

Always wash hands after handling earth.

Put caps on the tips of all canes and stakes, to avoid accidents.